THE COLOR PURPLE & ALL THAT JAZZ!

African American Achievements in the Arts

by Carole Marsh

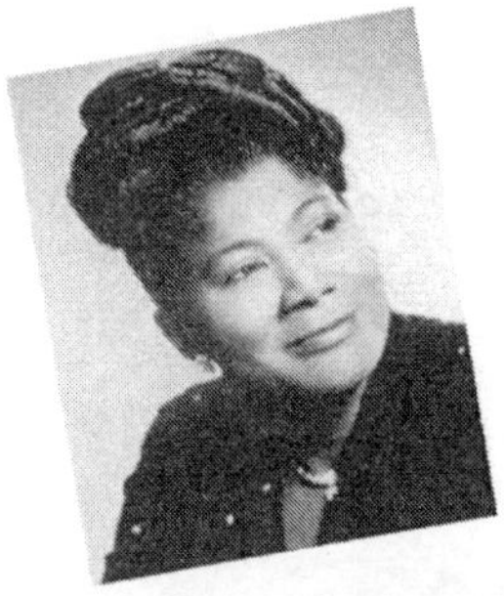

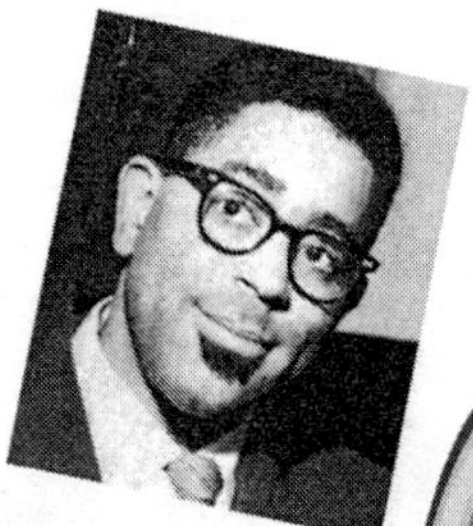

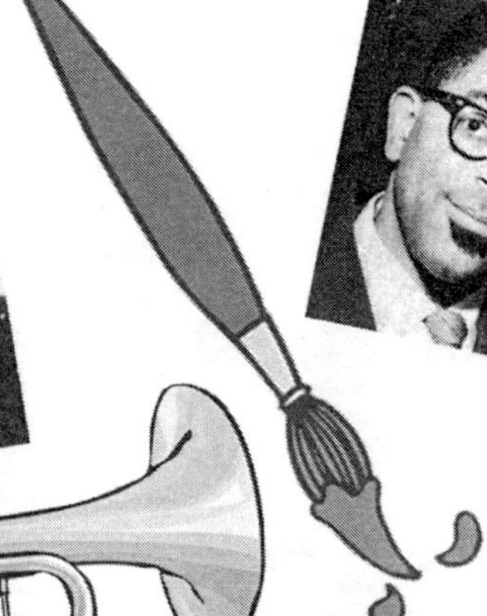

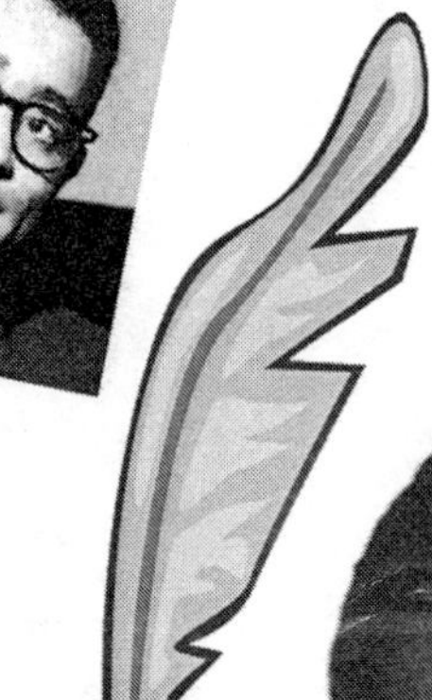

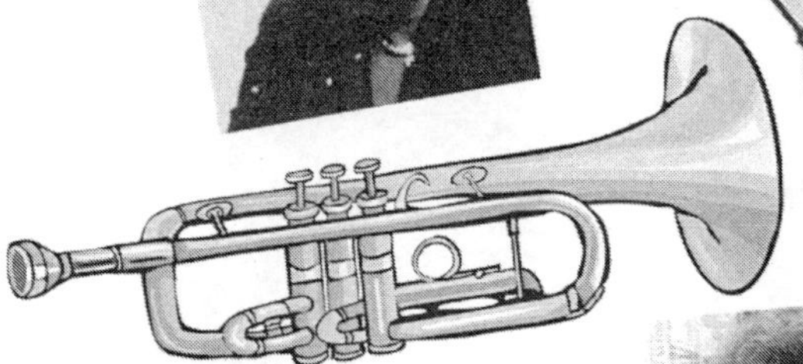

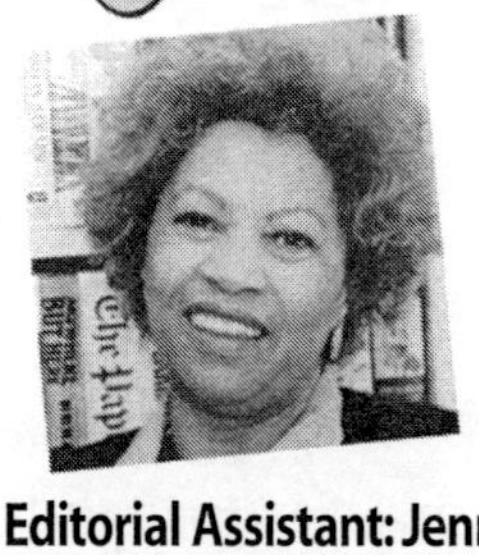

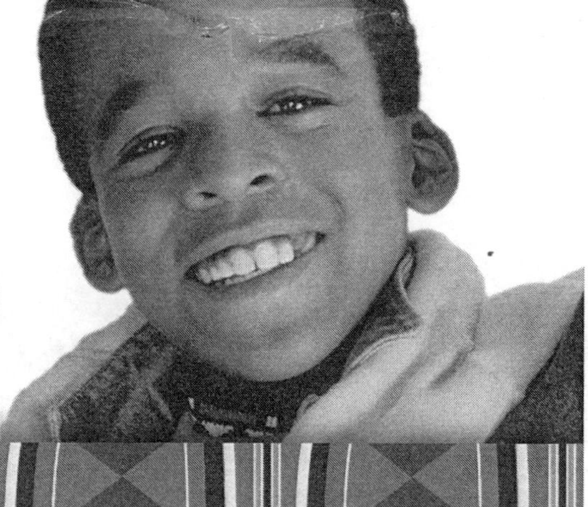

Black Jazz, Pizzazz & Razzmatazz™

Editorial Assistant: Jenny Corsey
Graphic Design: Cecil Anderson

Published by
GALLOPADE INTERNATIONAL
800-536-2GET
www.gallopade.com

Gallopade is proud to be a member of these educational organizations and associations:

The National School Supply and Equipment Association
The National Council for the Social Studies
Association for Supervision and Curriculum Development
Museum Store Association
Association of Partners for Public Lands

Black Jazz, Pizzazz, & Razzmatazz Books

Our Black Heritage Coloring Book

The Big Book of African American Activities

Black Heritage GameBook: Keep Score! Have Fun!
Find out how much you already know—and learn lots more!

Black Trivia: The African American Experience A-to-Z!

Celebrating Black Heritage:
20 Days of Activities, Reading, Recipes, Parties, Plays, and More!

Mini Timeline of Awesome African American Achievements and Events

"Let's Quilt Our African American Heritage & Stuff It Topographically!"

The Best Book of Black Biographies

"Out of the Mouths of Slaves": African American Oral History

The Kitchen House: How Yesterday's Black Women Created Today's
Most Popular & Famous American Foods!

Black Business: African American Entrepreneurs & Their Amazing Success!

Other Carole Marsh Books

Meet Shirley Franklin: Mayor of Atlanta!

African American Readers—Many to choose from!

Table of Contents

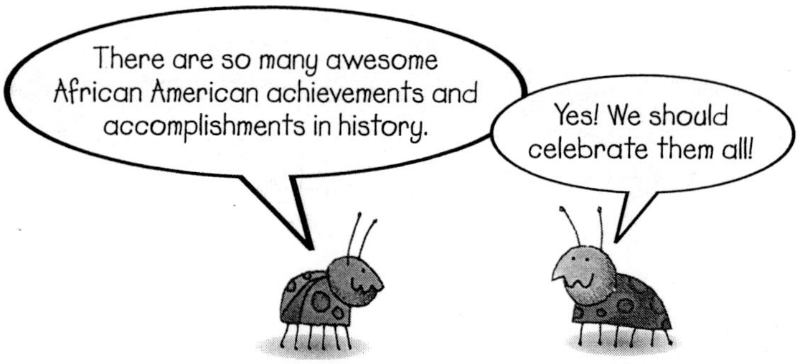

A Word From the Author

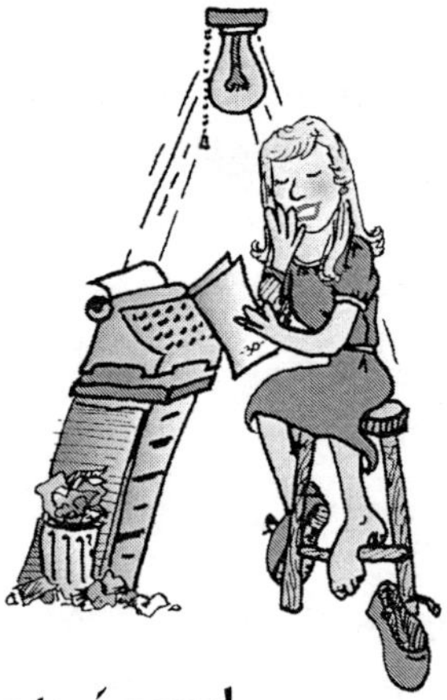

The color purple & all that jazz!

There must be a lot of ways to tell about the contribution of African Americans to the world of the arts. But this book, like many energetic artists, just starts right in!

This is just a sampling of the talent from the past and present. And with each printing, we hope to add the latest newcomers as they appear on the arts scene.

Hopefully, there are some forms of art that you especially enjoy. You do not have to be a great opera singer to sing, or an award-winning artist to paint, or a published writer to write. Everyone should make some form of art a part of their daily life—whether it's watching, supporting or doing.

If there is one theme that seems to connect this random sampling of black artists, it may be imagination and dedication. Black artists are extremely creative and seem unafraid to let their imaginations soar. And they never give up! No matter how hard the road or how many obstacles or potholes in it—they just keep on trying till they get it right.

Perhaps the most wonderful thing you'll discover is that some of the sweetest words come from the simplest things said by people who were not necessarily professionals. And professional or amateur, black art, like the color purple, is for sharing. We are all grateful for the contributions made and the joy they have brought to our lives... and all that kind of jazz!

Carole Marsh

OSCAR PETERSON

Canadian jazz pianist and composer

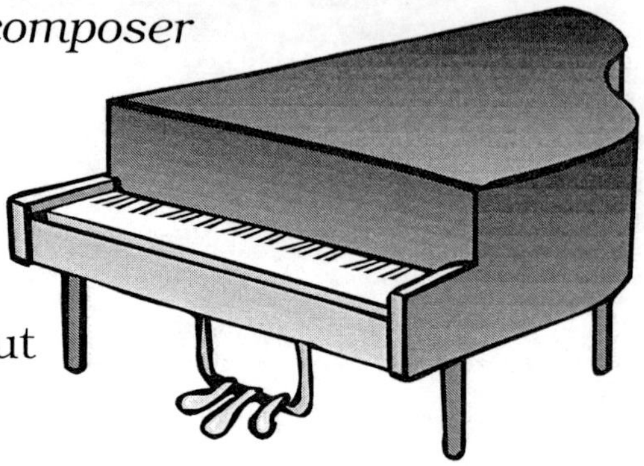

Oscar Peterson was born on August 15, 1925 in Montreal, Quebec, Canada. He was taught music first by his father, and then a private tutor. His first instrument was the trumpet, which he dearly loved, but was forced to give up after a year-long bout with tuberculosis.

His classical keyboard training enabled him to develop the hallmark of his performance—lightning right hand intricacies accompanied by swinging rhythm in the left. Singer Carmen McRae said of him, "There are many other pianists I love, but... Oscar is my favorite because he encompasses everything."

Peterson is the most recorded of all jazz pianists. He recorded over 200 albums and was a three-time Grammy Award winner. He got his first break in a CBC network radio talent contest at age 14. Five years later his first big hit was recorded: "I Got Rhythm" with "The Sheik of Araby" on the flip side. He gave a surprise performance at Carnegie Hall in New York City in 1949 during a concert featuring several famous jazz artists. His show-stopping performance drew a standing ovation and rave reviews. Between 1959 and 1963, he won first place in a readers' poll of the jazz magazine, *Down Beat*, eleven times. The remaining years he won similar acclaim in polls in *Metronome, Playboy* and *Le Jazz Hot*.

Peterson has high standards of performance. He refuses to play in uncontrolled settings. He calls himself "a stick-in-the-mud on [the] matter of the calibre of performance... You carry a responsibility on stage with you."

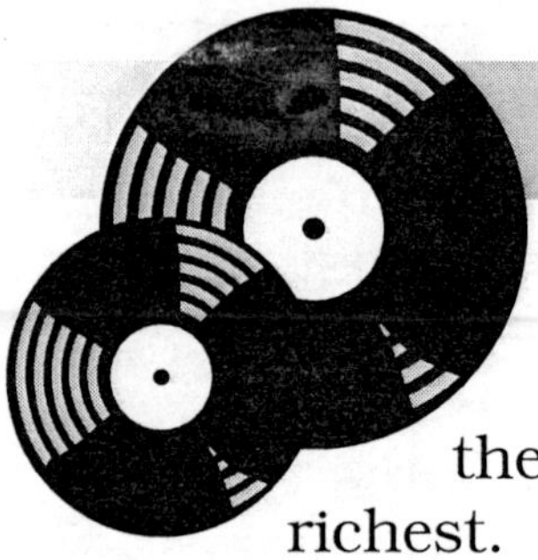

MICHAEL JACKSON

singer; dancer; songwriter and actor

At an early age, Michael Jackson had already become one of the most famous performers in the history of music—and one of the richest. He once completed a world tour to sell-out audiences which grossed $125,000,000. His soul/rock crossover album "Thriller" sold over 10,000,000 copies, setting a world record for non-soundtrack LPs in 1984.

Jackson was born into a musical family of performers in Gary, Indiana, on August 29, 1958. He was the fifth of nine children. The family also produced the Jackson Five and Jermaine, LaToya and Janet Jackson as solo artists. Born of musical parents, the children exhibited a natural talent and began to sing together spontaneously when their television set broke down. When they later added instruments, the Jackson Five began to perform publicly in the 1960s. At age five, Jackson was such an energetic little singer and dancer that he moved into the spotlight as lead. By age seven, he was choreographing for the whole group.

Jackson is famous for his unique, expressive singing and his dynamic dancing which exhilarates his audiences. Fans loved his silver glove and "moonwalk" dance. He says "On stage... I feel so free, so unlimited... like I can do anything... When I'm not on stage, I guess I'm quiet and shy. I sort of close down."

The singer has several children. Jackson is still fascinated with "magic," and identifies with Peter Pan his favorite fictional character. He has several exotic pets, a movie theater in his home, and a collection of life-size mannequins.

Jackson is known as one the greatest entertainers in the twentieth century, earning the title "King of Pop."

BILL COSBY

comedian; actor; author

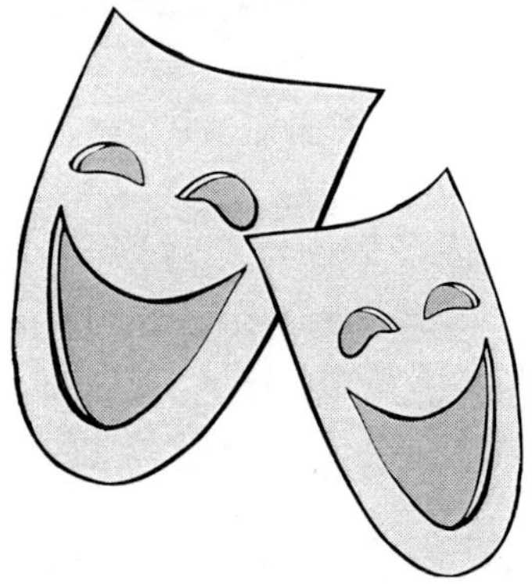

Bill Cosby, born William Henry Cosby, Jr., on July 12, 1937, is a rare comedian whose quarter-century career has placed him high on the entertainment scale for audiences of all races. His gentle humor revolves around the commonplace events that occur every day in a middle-class family, rather than the vulgar or racial jokes on which some comedians have built their careers.

Cosby grew up in an African American development in the Germantown district of North Philadelphia with his two younger brothers. He was always a comedian, inspired by Sid Caesar in particular, and did not study sufficiently to excel at school. He played basketball, baseball and football and was captain of the track and football teams. Rather than repeat the 10th grade, he dropped out of school and eventually enlisted in the U.S. Navy, where he learned physical therapy. After his four-year naval duty, Cosby enrolled at Temple University as a physical education major, where he was again active in sports.

The professional career as a comedian began when he was a sophomore and was hired for $5 as bartender and joke-teller at a coffeehouse. Later he filled in at another nightspot when the regular comedian had a night off. In the spring of 1962, he took a temporary leave from college to entertain at the Gaslight Cafe in New York's Greenwich Village. Soon after, he officially quit school to pursue a full-time career, touring all over the country.

Early in his career, Cosby told some racial jokes, but soon abandoned them because he wanted "to reach all the people." His material is his own creation and he enhances the joke-telling with funny faces, sound effects, and hilarious impersonations.

An appearance on the *Tonight Show* launched his acting career. He became a co-star on NBC's "I Spy," which ran for three years. Cosby earned three consecutive Emmy Awards for that role. His fourth Emmy came in 1969 for his "Bill Cosby Special." In September of that year, "The Bill Cosby Show" began its two-year run on NBC. Cosby not only starred, but co-directed and co-created the show, building it around the life he might have had if he had pursued the physical education degree.

After appearing in a couple of films, Cosby was back with a "New Bill Cosby Show," a comedy and variety program. At the same time, he enjoyed popularity with the younger set as a result of his Saturday morning cartoon series, "Fat Albert & The Cosby Kids." He also appeared frequently on "Sesame Street" and "Electric Company." Cosby's face could be seen quite often in television commercials, and all of America recognized him. Several films and an unsuccessful television series later, Cosby once more captured his audience with "The Cosby Show" in 1984. It has become one of the most popular comedies in television history. The show has been awarded the Emmy, the Gold Globe Award and a number of People's Choice Awards.

Cosby has written a book and recorded more than 20 record albums, which have sold millions and earned him eight Grammy Awards. He is also a spokesman for *Jello*. Cosby received the NAACP Image Award and the Spingarn Award.

HATTIE McDANIEL

radio and movie star

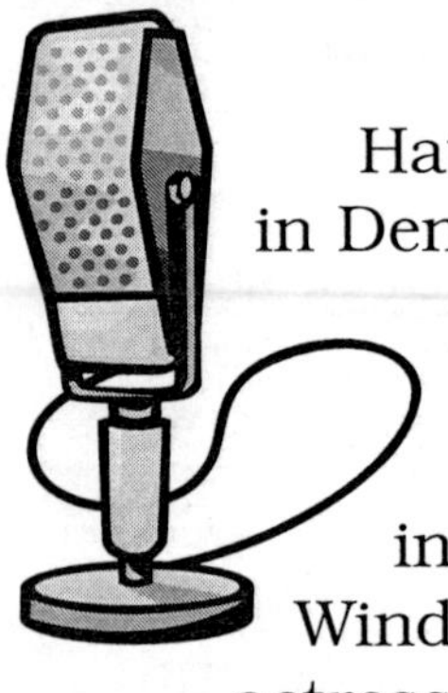

Hattie McDaniel was born June 10, 1898, in Wichita, Kansas, and lived in Denver, Colorado, as a youngster. She began her successful career by singing on Denver radio as an amateur. From there she moved into vaudeville as a professional and was a "headliner" by 1924. Moving to Hollywood in 1931, she appeared in several motion pictures, including "Showboat" and "Nothing Sacred." Her "Gone With The Wind" performance as "Mammy" earned her an Oscar for best supporting actress in 1940. McDaniel also enjoyed huge success on the radio as "Hi-Hat Hattie" and "Beulah." She died on October 26, 1952.

FAST FACT: Following her movie debut in 1932, Hattie McDaniel appeared in more than 300 different films over the next two decades.

SIDNEY POITIER

actor

Sidney Poitier was born in Miami, Florida, on February 20, 1924, but spent most of his childhood in the Bahamas. He returned to Miami at age sixteen, and shortly moved to New York, where he auditioned for the American Negro Theatre. He was turned down. He worked diligently on his diction and tried again. This time he was accepted and received acting lessons in exchange for backstage chores. Poitier was awarded the Oscar for Best Actor in 1963 for his portrayal of an itinerant construction worker in "Lilies of the Field." He was the first African American actor to have his hands and feet imprinted in the cement of Grauman's Chinese Theater in Hollywood. Poitier has appeared in numerous films, among them "No Way Out," "A Patch of Blue," "Guess Who's Coming to Dinner?," "A Raisin in the Sun," and "The Defiant Ones."

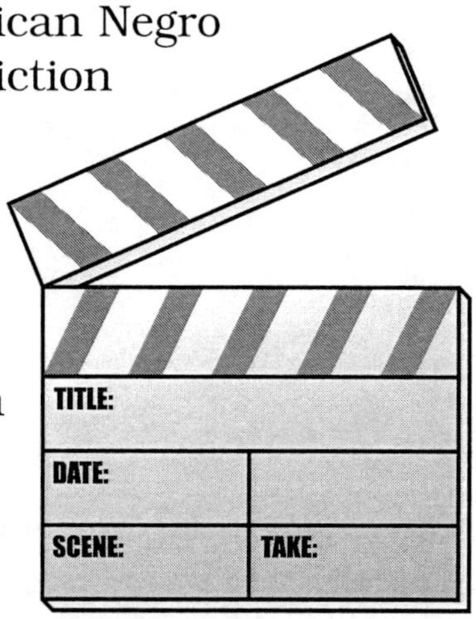

OPRAH WINFREY

talk show hostess; actress

Oprah Winfrey's screen debut in the 1985 Steven Spielberg film, "The Color Purple," was the beginning of something great. She was nominated for Academy and Golden Globe awards and was cast in another film, "Native Son." She has been a very successful talk show hostess since 1984. She was a precocious child who was often the entertainment at black social clubs and church teas, where she was known as "the little speaker." She had learned to entertain herself on the isolated farm where she lived with her maternal grandmother after the separation of her unmarried parents. A few years later, when she rejoined her mother, she lacked parental guidance and was abused by a series of trusted men. This left her guilt-ridden and confused.

After a dramatic demonstration of delinquency, her father took her to Nashville to live with him and his wife, Zelma. Oprah says he "saved her life." He was a strict, up-standing citizen who demanded respect and obedience. Under his strict guidance, she became an outstanding student and was involved in all sorts of extracurricular activities. She was crowned Miss Fire Prevention by WVOL, a local radio station, and was hired by the station to read newscasts. During her freshman year at Tennessee State University, Oprah was crowned Miss Black Nashville and Miss Tennessee. She relied on her poise and talent to compensate for what she terms her "fudge brownie" skin color.

She turned down a job offer from a CBS television station twice to continue with her college education, but at age 19 her speech teacher reminded her that job offers from CBS were the reason "people go to college." She accepted the position of co-anchor on the evening news on WTVF-TC, becoming the first African American woman to fill that position in Nashville. During her years as a newswoman, she labored under the stress of the insensitivity of the profession. People had their privacy invaded and sometimes things were so disturbing that she had a hard time controlling her emotions during the broadcast.

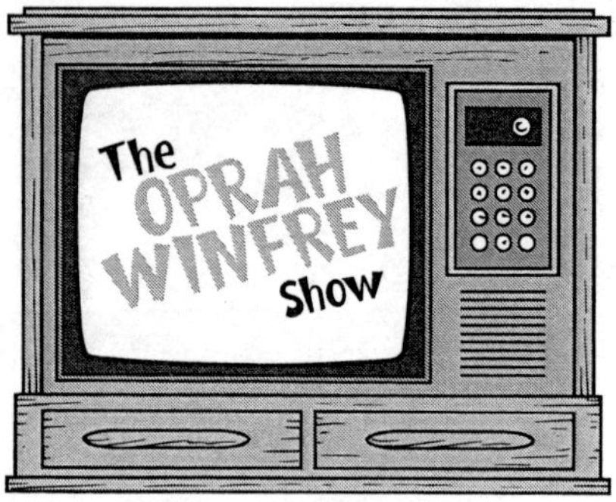

Today Oprah Winfrey is one of the highest paid performers in show business. She has not lost the caring concern she has always had for fellow human beings and their suffering. She lectures several nights a week, often *gratis*, at churches, shelters, and youth organizations, and spends two Saturdays a month with the Little Sisters program she set up at Chicago's notorious Cabrini-Green housing project. On January 23, 1987, WLS-TV and the Chicago *Sun-Times* launched a year-long anti-drug campaign called "Say No", and Oprah was host of their flagship program. She received a special award from the Chicago Academy for the Arts for her unique contributions to the city's artistic community. In August of 1986 she formed Harpo Inc. ("Oprah" spelled backwards) to produce "things [she] really [wants] to do." She says "When I look to the future, it's so bright it burns my eyes."

LOUIS ARMSTRONG

jazz trumpeter; music ambassador

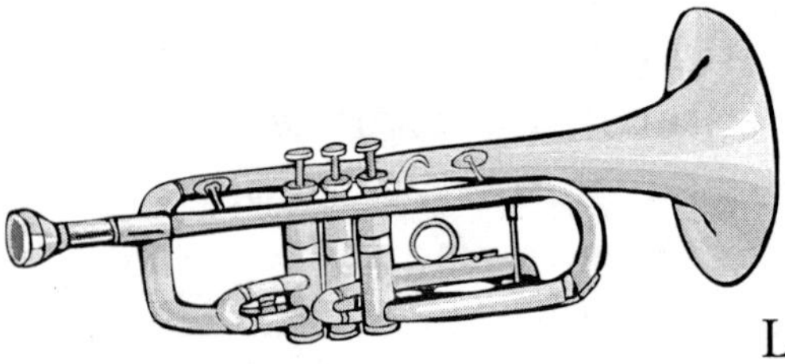

Louis Armstrong had a very humble beginning in New Orleans on the July 4, 1900. After the final departure of his father, his mother was forced to work full-time to support her small family, leaving Louis and his sister, Beatrice, on their own each day. Louis and four of his friends made themselves some instruments and began to play on the street for pennies. Louis always had holes in his pockets, so he'd hold his pennies in his mouth for safe-keeping. The kids started calling him "Satchelmouth," which later became his famous nickname, "Satchmo."

A few years later, when Louis was employed at a newsstand, his big interest was still music. He and his friends would follow bands to the cemetery every time there was a funeral and then dance their way back as the band played jazzy music on its return march.

After a mix-up with the police on New Year's Eve, Louis was placed in a Waif's House where he spent many unhappy days. The one bright spot was the Waif's Band, which practiced where he could hear. Eventually he was allowed to join them, finally getting the opportunity to play the bugle after the boy who played it was sent home. When Louis got his chance, he made it count, polishing the bugle until it shone and practicing so hard that the band teacher got him a shiny, golden cornet. He learned to play so well that he soon became the leader of the band. The band became very popular as local entertainment for picnics and social gatherings. It was a great treat for Louis when they played in the old neighborhood. He would proudly stand up front and lead the band with his cornet.

When Louis turned 14, he was sent home. He was so sad at leaving the band and his cornet that he cried. Now that he was "a man," he became the family's support, working two jobs to make ends meet. By day he delivered coal, but by night he was a jazz musician! Since he couldn't afford a horn, his boss got one for him from a pawn shop. He began his long and successful career by making 50¢ a night. He couldn't read notes very well, but he had a great ear and especially loved to play blues, ragtime, jazz spirituals, and funeral marches.

Once when he had a sore lip, Louis sang part of his trumpet part. His raspy, gruff voice inspired so much audience response, that he made it a regular part of his act. Louis gained great popularity and played with every great band and jazz musician in the country. He was known as the "Ambassador of Jazz," and he attributed his success to his smile and his originality.

KATHLEEN BATTLE

Operatic Singer

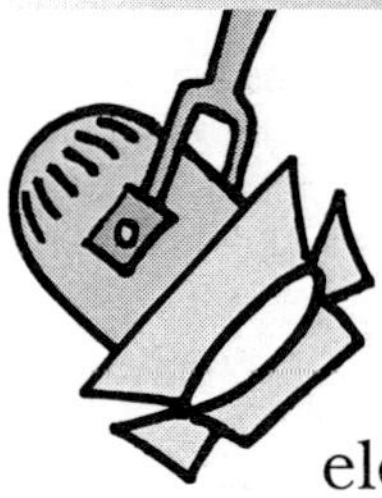

Universally acclaimed by her peers for what one of them called her "special quality of communicating with the public" as well as for her superlative voice, Kathleen Battle began her professional life teaching elementary school in an African American ghetto in Cincinnati, Ohio. She made her singing debut in 1972 at the Spoleto (Italy) Festival of Two Worlds and went on to earn critics' praise in several world music capitals.

The last of the seven children of Grady Battle, a steelworker, and his wife, Ollie (Lane) Battle, Kathleen Deanne Battle was born on August 13, 1948 in Portsmouth, Ohio, a small industrial city in southern Ohio. Her siblings—three brothers and three sisters—include a teacher, an accountant, a welder, a secretary, a carpenter, and a personnel supervisor. "It's a wonderfully close family, which gives the strength," Miss Battle told Peter Goodman of *Newsday* [March 25, 1984]. "Maybe you don't appreciate it much growing up, when you have to share beds, bedrooms, closets, but you do... more later on."

A diligent and hard-working child, Kathleen Battle excelled in all her subjects at the local public school. Consequently, when she began piano lessons at the age of twelve, her special aptitude for music was not immediately noticed. In high school, she took secretarial courses in typing and shorthand.

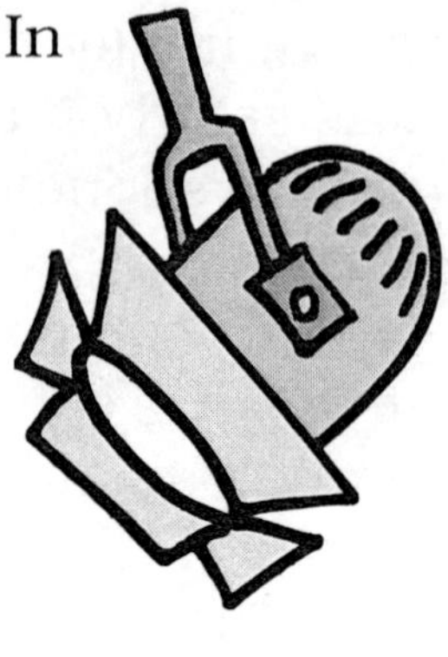

Despite her love of music and her undeniable signing talent, the idea of a career in the performing arts did not occur to her. "I'm sure that anyone who studies singing hears people saying they have a lovely voice," she told Mark Steinbrink, as quoted in the *New York Times* [May 2, 1982]. "I always just thought the people were being kind."

On her graduation from Portsmouth High School in 1966, Miss Battle was awarded a Ford Foundation National Achievement Scholarship. Persuaded by her high school music teacher to major in music instead of mathematics, she enrolled at the College-Conservatory of Music at the University of Cincinnati, but she decided against specializing in performance, opting instead for music education.

In 1971, her bachelor's and master's degrees in music education from the University of Cincinnati in hand, Miss Battle began teaching fifth and sixth grade at the Garfield School in Cincinnati's inner city. In the evenings, she took second-year German and studied voice with Franklin Bens, who focused on oratorio literature. After studying privately for a year, she auditioned for Thomas Schippers, who was the director of the Cincinnati Symphony Orchestra. Although her previous performing experience consisted of little more than singing in local church choirs, Schippers immediately hired Miss Battle to sing the soprano part in Brahm's *Ein Deutsches Requiem*, as well as several Handel arias, at the 1972 Spoleto festival.

Returning to Cincinnati in the fall of 1972, Miss Battle continued to teach music at the elementary school level, but she agreed to repeat her performance of *Ein Deutsches Requiem* for a Cincinnati Symphony Orchestra concert.

Earlier in her career, Miss Battle had occasionally felt that she was in over her head, but by the 1981-1982 season, she clearly found her stride, as John Rockwell of the *New York Times* observed. "She is rapidly developing into one of our most valuable artists—a pure, radiant soprano linked to a sensitive interpretive personality."

FAST FACT: Concert performer Marian Anderson was the first African American to sing a main role with the Metropolitan Opera in 1955. She toured around Europe to perform in various concert halls. Marian was also the first African American, along with Ralph Bunche, to win a Presidential Medal of Freedom in 1963!

WILLIAM H. CARNEY

Civil War Infantryman

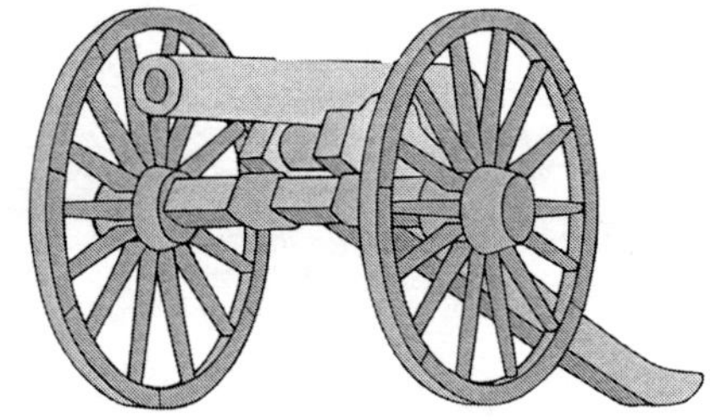

Sergeant William H. Carney was born in New Bedford, Massachusetts. In 1863, he became the first Negro to win the Congressional Medal of Honor for his heroism in the Battle of Fort Wagner. Against tremendous odds, he held his regimental colors high, even though he was severely wounded twice. He is quoted as saying "The old flag never touched the ground, boys." The following poem is in remembrance of his heroic deed:

THE OLD FLAG NEVER TOUCHED THE GROUND

"The Old Flag never touched the ground!" 'twas thus brave Carney spoke,
A Negro soldier: words renowned, that Honor will invoke
Upon the records of the Race whose heroes many are,
Records that Time cannot efface, and Hate can never mar.
Those words were stamped with Carney's blood upon our Country's scroll,
And though dislike, deep as a flood, against his Race may roll,
It cannot dim, nor wash away, its crimson-written fame
Which History wrote on Wagner's day without a tinge of shame.
Not only Carney did she view, when with immortal pen
She stood to write the honors due one thousand Colored men
Who laughed at death, who felt no fear, and followed Colonel Shaw
Where none but heroes dared to go, with cheer and loud hurrah.
July the eighteenth, of the year eighteen-and-sixty-three,
To Negroes always will be dear, as any one could be,
For bloody cost of honors won, for loss of noble life,
For valor that no risk would shun in fiercest battle strife.

The ACHIEVEMENTS...

of women in the arts.

1746 **Lucy Terry (Prince)**, (1730-1821), America's first slave poetess, writes *Bars Fight*, which is hailed as the most authentic account of the Deerfield Massacre, an Indian raid in Massachusetts.

1773 **Phillis Wheatley**, (1753-1784), a slave, writes *Poems On Various Subjects, Religious and Moral*, one of the first two books of verse by an American woman.

1821 The first recorded professional theatrical performance staged by blacks includes women performers and is presented by the **New York City African Company**.

1843 **Sojourner Truth**, (1797-1883), begins speaking for the abolitionist cause. She draws large crowds and soon gains widespread popularity because of her dynamic personality and her gifts of wit and song.

1851 **Elizabeth Taylor Greenfield**, (1819-1876), appears in concert for the first time in New York. Three years later she will sing at Buckingham Palace and be praised by the London press for her performances.

1859 **Harriet E. Adams Wilson**, (1827-1870), was the first black woman to publish a novel.

Frances Ellen Watkins Harper, (1825-1911), publishes her first short story, which appeared in *Anglo-American* magazine. She becomes the first black woman in the U.S. to do so.

1864 The first black woman to gain widespread recognition as an artist, **Edmonia Lewis**, (1845-1890), exhibits sculpture at the Soldiers Aid Fair in Boston.

1888 Gifted soprano, **Sissieretta Jones**, (1868-1933), makes her public debut in New York. She later sings opera with her own traveling theater company.

1890 A female chorus appears in the all-black production, *The Creole Show.*

1895 Black women appear in leading roles in John Isham's play, *The Octoroon.*

1900 The first black female blues singer, **Gertrude Pridgett "Ma" Rainey**, (1886-1939), makes her debut performance at the Springer Opera House in Columbus, Georgia.

1905 Vocalist, **Abbie Mitchell**, (1884-1960), appears with the first modern jazz band in New York City.

THE HARLEM RENAISSANCE

In Northern urban centers, black communities grow in pride and self-awareness, which nurtures creativity. Black music, literature, drama, dance, and art flourish.

1920 **Mamie Smith,** (1883-1946), records "Crazy Blues." Her success opens the recording industry to other black musicians.

1921 **Florence Mills**, (1896-1927), stars in the successful all-black Broadway musical extravaganza, *Shuffle Along.*

1923 **Bessie Smith**, (1894-1937), makes her first recording, ***"Down Hearted Blues"*** (written by Alberta Hunter). This record sells 780,000 copies in less than six months and Smith becomes known as the "Empress of the Blues."

1925 The dynamic entertainer, **Josephine Baker**, (1906-1975), becomes the first black to star in a solo revue on the Paris stage.

Outstanding portrait painter and illustrator, **Laura Wheeler Waring**, (1887-1948), exhibits at the Philadelphia Exposition.

1927 The controversial and free-spirited writer, **Zora Neale Hurston**, (1891-1960), begins research in African American folklore in Harlem, New York City and the South.

1930 **Mahalia Jackson**, (1911?-1972), forms the Johnson Gospel Singers. In a few years, she receives invitations to sing in black churches from New York to California.

1935 The great jazz singer, **Billie Holiday**, (1915-1959) records with Teddy Johnson and his band and is favorably reviewed.

After working in cotton fields and cooking on a plantation where many artists congregate, **Clementine Hunter**, (1886-1988), begins experimenting with paints left behind by guests.

1938 Gospel singer, **Sister Rosetta Tharpe**, (1921-1973), appears in John Henry Hammond's ***From Spirituals to Swing*** at Carnegie Hall.

Entertainer, **Lena Horne,** (b. 1917), is featured for the first time on Broadway in *Blackbirds*.

Jazz vocalist, **Ella Fitzgerald**, (1918-1996) becomes the leader of Chick Webb's band after his death.

1940 Artist, **Elizabeth Catlett**, (b. 1919), exhibits at the American Negro Exposition in Chicago.

Katherine Dunham, (b. 1912), a dancer, choreographer, and anthropologist, is widely acclaimed when her ***Tropics and Le Jazz Hot: From Haiti to Harlem*** is performed at New York's Windsor Theater.

The SUCCESS CONTINUES...

1942 **Margaret Walker**, (1915-1998), wins the Yale Award for Young Poets for her moving collection of poems, ***For My People***, "Let a new earth rise. Let another world be born. Let a bloody peace be written in the sky..."

1943 **Dinah Washington**, (1924-1963), who becomes one of the most popular singers of rhythm and blues, gets her first big break, a job with Lionel Hampton.

1946 **Mary Lou Williams**, (1910-1981), the leading female jazz instrumentalist (piano) plays her composition, "Zodiac Suite," with the New York Philharmonic Orchestra.

Actress, **Ruby Dee**, (b. 1924), appears on Broadway for the first time in ***Jeb***.

1947 Performer and choreographer, **Pearle Primus**, (1919-1994), opens a school of dance in New York City.

1950 **Gwendolyn Brooks**, (1917-2000), is the first African American to win a Pulitzer Prize for her book of poetry, ***Annie Allen***.

1959 **Lorraine Hansberry's**, (1930-1965), award-winning ***A Raisin in the Sun***, is the first play authored by an African American woman to be produced on Broadway.

1961 Artist, writer, educator, **Margaret Burroughs**, (b. 1917), founds the DuSable Museum of Afro-American History, Inc., in Chicago.

1967 "Queen of Soul" **Aretha Franklin**, (b. 1942), records four gold singles.

1969 Painter and illustrator, **Lois Mailou Jones**, (1905-1998), is awarded a grant by Howard University to study contemporary art in Haiti.

1970 Popular poet and public speaker, **Nikki Giovanni** (b. 1943) publishes ***Black Feeling***, ***Black Talk***, ***Black Judgment***.

Writer, **Toni Morrison**, (b. 1931), known for her use of black dialect, publishes her first novel, ***The Bluest Eye***.

1972 Actress, **Cicely Tyson**, (b. 1942), appears as an African American heroine in the film, ***Sounder***.

1977 **Varnette P. Honeywood**, (b. 1950), is one of the African American artists to go to Lagos, Nigeria, as a participant in FESTAC, an international festival of black arts and culture.

1983 **Alice Walker**, (b. 1944), becomes the first African American to win the Pulitzer Prize in fiction for her novel, *The Color Purple*. The work also won an American Book Award. Walker writes poetry, essays, and fiction.

1993 **Maya Angelou**, (b. 1928), becomes the first African American inaugural poet at President Bill Clinton's inauguration. She read her poem "On the Pulse of Morning" for the occasion. She has also been an actress, dancer and movie director.

1993 **Halle Berry**, (b. 1968), becomes the first African American to win Best Actress. The award honored her portrayal of the 1950s black movie star **Dorothy Dandridge**.

2002 Talk show host **Oprah Winfrey** receives the first Bob Hope Humanitarian Award at the 54th annual Emmy Awards.

QUOTES & FACTS

"This thing is beautiful. Destroy not this beauty, this singing around the world."
— **Joseph Shambalala,** Ladysmith Black Mambazo leader

As a child, African American author **James Baldwin** wrote on paper bags because his family couldn't afford paper.

Author **Claude Brown** wrote ***Manchild in the Promised Land***, a story about growing up in Harlem, a section of New York City. He used to beg his friends to teach him to play hooky. "You have to go to school first!" they told him.

James William Charles Pennington, (1807-1870), authored the first history of the black people written from an African American perspective. A minister, Pennington performed the ceremony at the wedding of Frederick Douglass.

George Moses Horton...

was a professional poet who supported himself during most of his life partly from the sale of his work. He was born a slave in Northampton County, North Carolina about 1797. Although he could not read or write, he began composing poems in his head to the meter of hymns he had heard in church. Students at the university heard his work, and with the faculty taught him to read and write. Using money he earned from selling his poetry, Horton paid his master for temporary freedom so he could live in Chapel Hill. However, he was still a slave.

Three books of his were published: *The Hope of Liberty*, *Poetical Works*, and *Naked Genius*. Protesting his status as a slave, The *Hope of Liberty* was the first book by a Negro in the South. The three volumes contain political and philosophical verses, love poems and other humorous selections. Horton called himself an "illiterate genius."

In 1865 when Union troops invaded North Carolina, Horton escaped to their lines and was free at last. A Yankee captain helped him with the publication of his final book. Horton moved to Philadelphia and became quite a celebrity there. But life in the North was not so easy-going as in the South, and soon he had to seek other kinds of work. Horton died about 1883.

Charles Waddell Chesnutt...

was a well known Southern African American author. At a time when other blacks in America were mostly indifferent to literature, Chesnutt made a name for himself in open competition with the best of the white authors.

At age 14, Chesnutt sold a story to a black newspaper. His career had begun! He taught in public schools and also served as principal. However, the discouraging Reconstruction Era was not favorable for the advancement of young black men. Chesnutt resented the prejudice so much that he moved to the North.

In New York, he worked as a newspaperman and then moved to Cleveland, Ohio. There he worked as a court reporter, stenographer, lawyer, lecturer, and was a respected citizen. Mark Twain, William Dean Howells, Walter Hines Page, Booker T. Washington, and others admired and advised him. Chesnutt died in 1932.

Samm-Art Williams...

was a famous dramatist and entertainment writer. After graduating from Morgan State University in Baltimore, he went to Philadelphia, then on to New York to break into theater. By 1974, he was a member of the Negro Ensemble Company as actor, director, and dramatist. Williams' 1979 play *Home* produced his greatest recognition.

In *Home*, Cephus, the main character, is a strong believer in God and in the land he tills beside the "White Stocking River" at "Cross Roads," North Carolina. When anything goes wrong, Cephus tells himself that God must be on vacation in Miami. A man of integrity — his grandfather and his Uncle Lewis had taught him the precepts "Thou shall not kill" and "Love thy neighbor" — Cephus refuses to go soldiering in Vietnam and is sent to prison in Raleigh, North Carolina.

When he is released, he heads North to work in a city, but the seven years he spends there are disappointing and degrading. "I love the land," he reminds himself and takes a bus home on Christmas Eve to see his sweetheart, Pattie Mae. His eyes lifted toward heaven, he speaks to his Lord, "You finally came back from Miami. Welcome Home."

The play enjoyed long runs on and off Broadway and toured widely across the country. The *New York Times* called *Home* "a play from the heart, about the heartline of America." Samm-Art Williams wrote other dramas, authored a television series, and acted in several Hollywood motion pictures.

The *Triumphs of Ephraim* (1907), by **James Ephraim McGirt**, (1890-1975), a black poet, depicts the black man in his struggle for improvement.

Frank Yerby, (1916-1991), becomes first best-selling American black novelist.

Alabama native and black poet **Gerald W. Barrax** (b. 1933) has taught creative writing and black studies since 1967. His books are titled *Another Kind of Rain* (1970) and *An Audience of One* (1980).

Toni Morrison, (b. 1931), first African American novelist to win a Pulitzer Prize in literature for her novel, *Beloved.*

Atlanta newspaperman, **Joel Chandler Harris**, (1848-1908), was one of the first writers of Negro folk literature. He created the characters Br'er Rabbit and the Tar Baby. What is a more popular name for Mr. Harris? **Answer: Uncle Remus!**

Countee Cullen, (1903-1946), was a great poet during the Harlem Renaissance.

Tobe was a story written by **Stella Gentry Sharpe** in 1939. It is the realistic story of a young black boy and his family on a North Carolina farm. The book used photographs instead of illustrations to show Tobe's life, a unique idea during that era.

James A. McPherson, (b. 1943), is an African American Pulitzer Prize-winning author. His collections of short stories are titled *Hue and Cry: Short Stories* and *Elbow Room: Stories.*

The Conjure Woman was a book of seven black folk tales written by **Charles Waddell Chestnut,** (1868-1932).

Gwendolyn Brooks, (1917-2000), was an acclaimed black poet from Chicago who became the first black to win a Pulitzer Prize for poetry with *Annie Allen.*

Carl T. Rowan, (1925-2000) prize-winning journalist; director of the U.S. Information Agency, 1964, the first African American to sit on the National Security Council; U.S. ambassador to Finland, 1963.

Paul Laurence Dunbar, (1872-1906), poet, novelist; won fame with *Lyrics of Lowly Life* in 1896.

THE NORTH CAROLINA BLACK REPERTORY COMPANY

Larry Leon Hamlin founded this theatre company in 1979. He directed almost 70 productions during his career. But he is probably most proud of the 1989 Black Theatre Festival that he organized in Winston-Salem, North Carolina.

Hamlin was born in Reidsville and learned how to act from his mother. His first theatrical experience came during the very first year of elementary school. He was supposed to recite a four-line poem before an audience of parents, teachers and students.

Even though he was nervous, he did his poem without a hitch. That is until the audience began to applaud his performance. That was the only time he forgot something. He forgot to leave the stage! Finally, a teacher dragged him off. But later he couldn't resist coming back to the stage and grabbing hold of those wonderful, bright, HOT spotlights! "I wish someone had warned me," he said.

In high school, he participated in the drama club and played a lead role in his first play, *It's Great to be Crazy*.

During college, he sold fire extinguishers to help pay his way. He did such a good job that he bought the company. But he soon discovered that business success did not make him happy. What would? The stage!

So, he sold his company, took acting lessons, and later directed more than 150 productions. His acting career spanned stage, television, and film.

When he returned to North Carolina, there were no professional black theatres, so he founded one. Hamlin thinks doing what you love and are good at is far more important than making money.

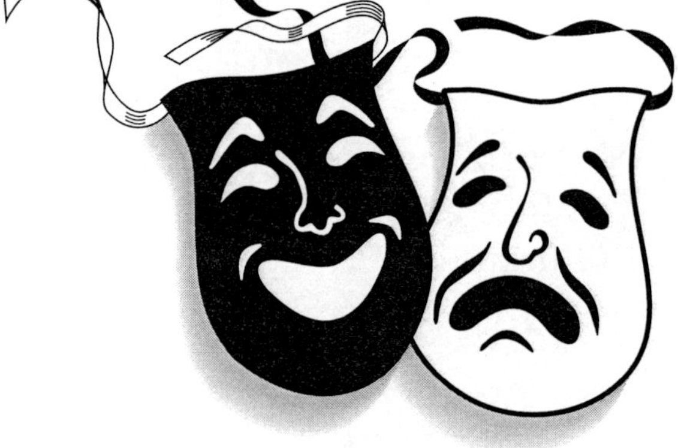

PHILDANCO

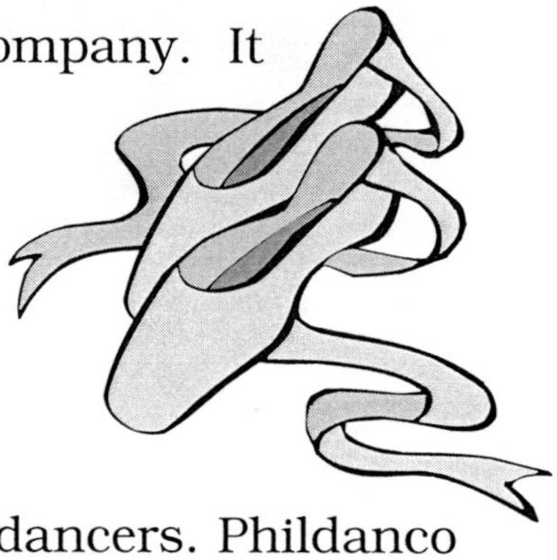

PHILDANCO is better known as the Philadelphia Dance Company. It was founded in 1970 by **Joan Myers Brown** as a performing company for minority students.

For a long time, the only way for a black dancer to make a living was in showdancing or nightclubs. Blacks were not accepted as "serious" dancers.

Phildanco helped provide prospects for African American dancers. Phildanco includes a performing company, training and instruction, and a children's program.

Brown thinks the discipline of dance is very good for young people. At the end of class, even though the dancers are exhausted, they must stand perfectly still. "When there may be only one place for a dancer and 500 dancers are auditioning, this extra discipline comes in handy," she says.

Why Philadelphia? Because Brown was born and raised there, went to school there, and wanted to give something back to the people in her hometown.

LADYSMITH BLACK MAMBAZO

Ladysmith Black Mambazo is not a lady. It's South Africa's most famous musical group. The group toured in America to help make people more aware of the terrible things going on in their homeland. One of their most popular albums, *Journey of Dreams*, is of lively Zulu songs. Their name can be translated as Black Axe of Ladysmith, meaning that they "cut down" their competition in every local singing contest.

You might know LBM better for the song *Graceland*, which the group did with Paul Simon. The group's leader is Joseph Shambalala. The type of music they play is called *Isicathamiya* (pronounced ITH SCOT TA MIA), which means "to walk lightly on one's toes."

If you hear LBM, you may find yourself stamping, clapping, cheering, laughing and crying — all at the same time! But it also reminds you of the situation in South Africa and the hope that things will soon change for the better.

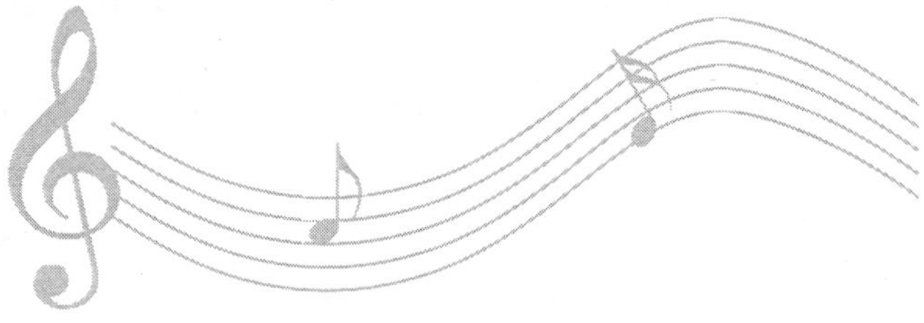

THE CHUCK DAVIS AFRICAN AMERICAN DANCE ENSEMBLE

The **Chuck Davis African American Dance Ensemble** performs authentic West African tribal dances. Their promise is "peace, love and respect for everybody." The group participates in many festivals!

QUICK QUESTIONS

Which fine art interests you?

____

If you could be an artist, what type would you be?

____

If you wrote a book, about what would you write?

____

If you painted a picture, what would you paint?

____

If you sculpted, what would you carve?

____

If you danced, what dance would you choose? What song would you select?

____

____

What black art do you have hanging in your home or classroom?
Do an inventory!

____

____

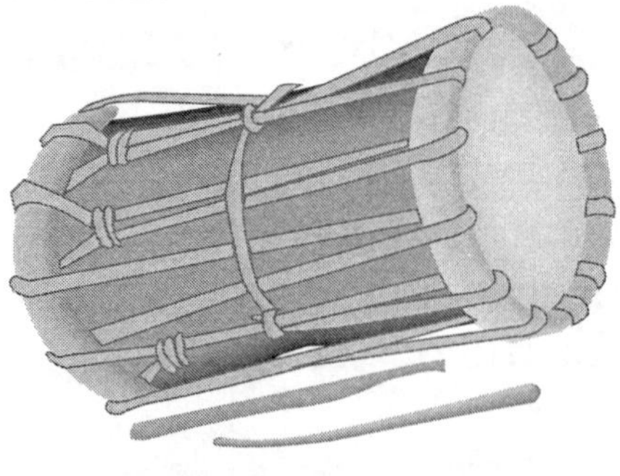

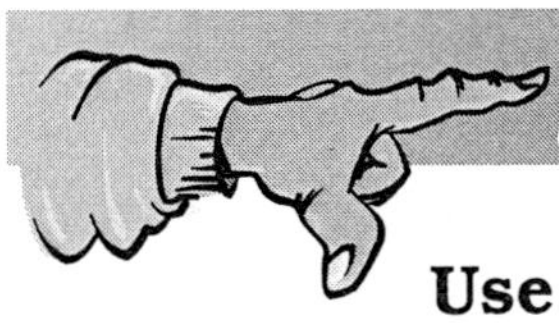

AWESOME ART "FIRSTS"

Use the answer bank to circle the correct answer in each question.

1. Ira Aldridge was the first black international (drama/dance/chef) star.

2. William Wells Brown was the first black (actor/novelist/artist).

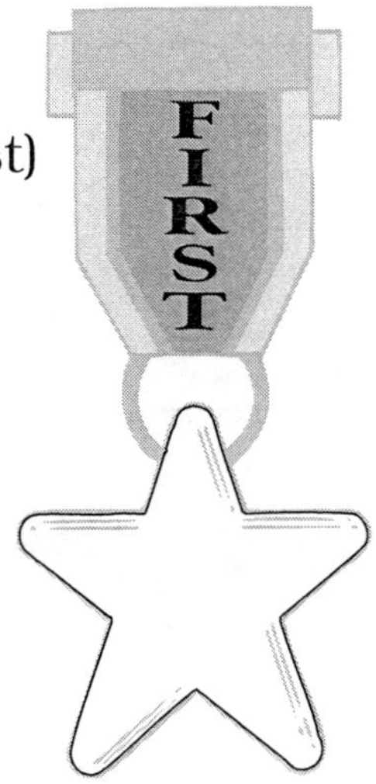

3. Marian Anderson was the first black (soloist/chorus girl/violinist) at the Metropolitan Opera.

4. The "Ed Sullivan Show" was the first (radio/television/Internet) series to regularly feature black artists.

5. W.C. Handy first published (blues/greens/purples).

6. Gwendolyn Brooks was the first black to win a Pulitzer Prize for (literature/poetry/essays).

7. Bert Williams was the first black (Broadway/Hollywood/Disney) star.

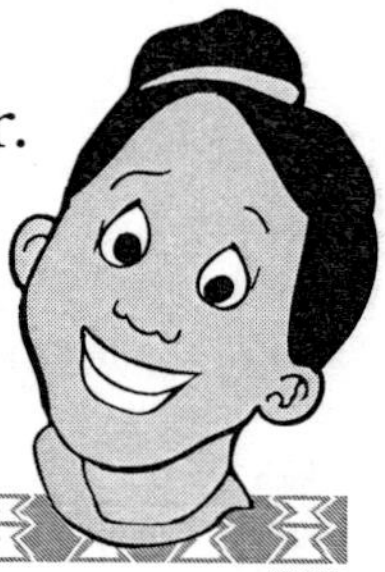

8. Roland Hayes was the first popular (white/black/gray) concertist.

ANSWER BANK

blues black television poet

Broadway poetry American

drama soloist novelist

Answers: 1. drama; 2. novelist; 3. soloist; 4. television; 5. blues; 6. poetry; 7. Broadway; 8. black

FACTS ABOUT FIRSTS:

Fine Art

The first black portrait painter to become well known in America was **Joshua Johnston** of Baltimore, Maryland. He was listed among "Free Householders of Color" in the 1796 Baltimore Directory. You can still see his work hanging in that town's museums.

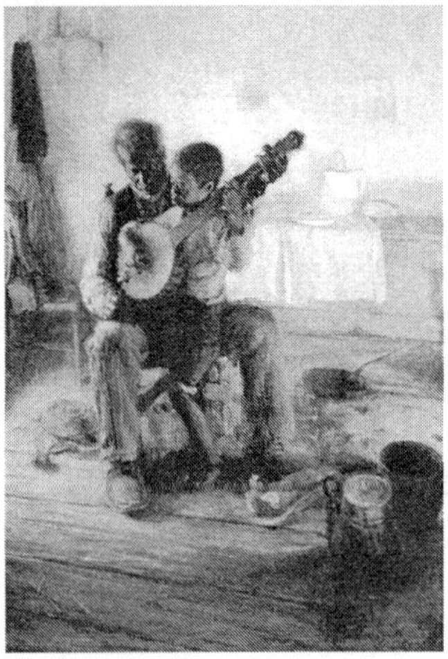

The Banjo Lesson by Henry O. Tanner

The first black artist to make a living from his work was **Henry O. Tanner**. He lived in Pittsburgh and Philadelphia, Pennsylvania, Atlanta, Georgia, and France. He was best known for his religious paintings.

Robert Bannister was the first black to achieve recognition as a regional painter. He lived and worked in Providence, Rhode Island. *Sabin Point, Narrangansett Bay* and *After the Storm* are some of his more famous landscapes.

The first black sculptor to achieve widespread appreciation in America was **Edmonia Lewis**. As an orphan, she was raised by Indians. She studied in Rome, Italy. Her best known works are *Hiawatha, Hagar in the Wilderness, Madonna and Child*, and *The Death of Cleopatra*.

Drama

The first black drama group in America was the **New York City African Company** which was started in 1821. They performed Shakespeare works and other classic plays. Even though the audience was mostly blacks, the theatre "graciously made a partition at the back of the house for the accommodation of whites."

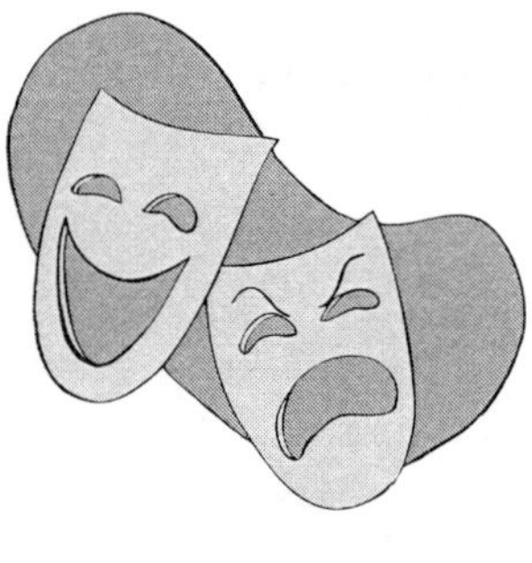

Appearances by **Garland Anderson** was the first Broadway play written by an African American. Before becoming a playwright, Garland worked as a bellhop in San Francisco, California. When his play opened in New York, he was greeted by the mayor in front of City Hall.

Paul Robeson was the first black to play the lead role in Shakespeare's *Othello* in America with an all-white cast. Robeson became internationally known on stage and in films.

Literature

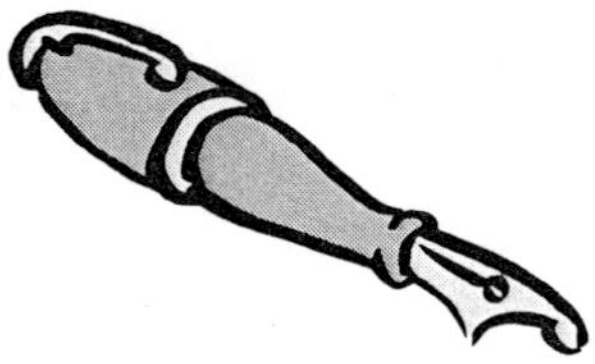

Paul Laurence Dunbar has been called the "poet laureate of the black race." His parents had been former slaves, and he was the only black student in his high school graduating class in Dayton, Ohio. He had the opportunity to read his poetry at the 1893 Chicago World's Fair and during Queen Victoria's Diamond Jubilee in London, England.

The first black detective novel was written by **Rudolph Fisher**. *The Conjure-Man Dies* was published in 1932.

Dance

Did you know the following dances all have their roots in black Africa? The ***rumba***, ***conga***, ***mambo***, ***tango***, ***samba***, ***Black Bottom***, and the ***cakewalk***? The ***rumba*** depicts simple farm chores. The samba is the national dance of Brazil and comes from a wedding dance in Angola, called the ***Quizomba***. The Black Bottom is still popular in Charleston, South Carolina. Do people still dance these dances? They sure do! Ask your parents if they can tango. Ask your grandparents!

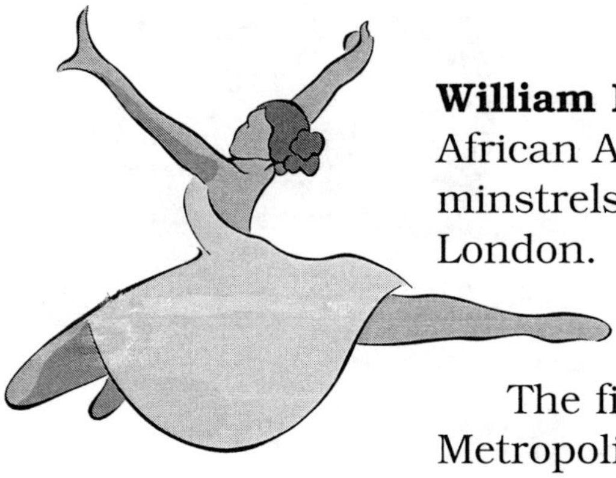

William Henry Lane, known as "Master Juba," was the first African American dance star. He toured abroad with white minstrels and was acclaimed in 1848 for a performance in London.

The first African American choreographer at the Metropolitan Opera House was **Katherine Dunham**. She became famous around the world for the artistic dances she created. **Arthur Mitchell** was the first black to join the New York City Ballet. And the **Alvin Ailey Dance Company** was the first black dance group to tour Russia. Before becoming a dancer, Ailey had been a star athlete in high school.

Janet Collins was the first African American ballerina at the Metropolitan Opera Company. Her dancing debut occurred during the ballet ***Adia***. She graduated from Los Angeles City College and Arts Centers School. Later, she taught dance.

THE MUSIC MAN

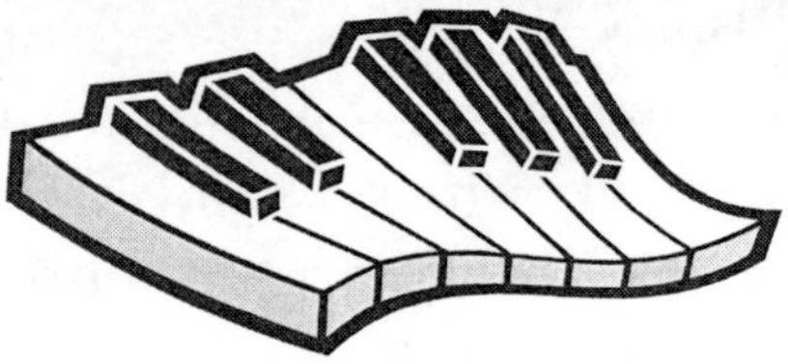

Use answer bank to write the correct answers in the blanks for each question.

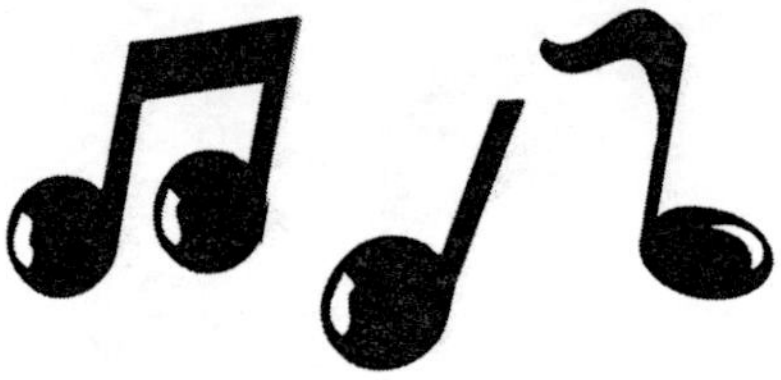

1. Duke Ellington was nicknamed "The ___ ___ ___ ___."

2. Thomas Bethune, who was born a blind slave in Georgia, became America's first black ___ ___ ___ ___ ___ ___ ___ to achieve national fame.

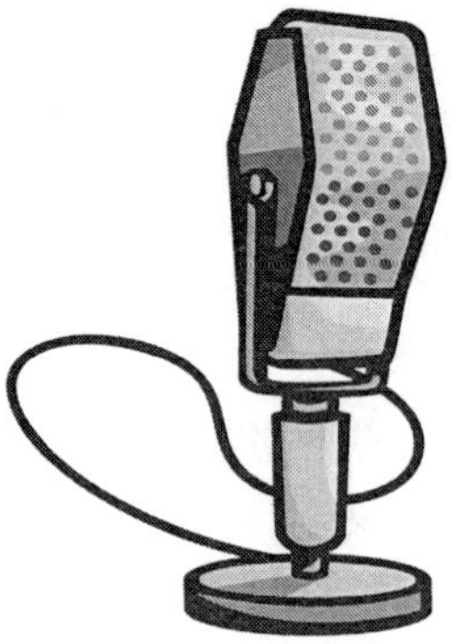

3. Symphony No. I was a black ___ ___ ___ ___ symphony.

4. J.J. Johnson played trombone in the hard "___ ___ ___" style.

5. Jazz first originated in New ___ ___ ___ ___ ___ ___ ___.

6. James Bland ___ ___ ___ ___ ___ the song, "Carry Me Back to Old Virginny."

7. Old spiritual or gospel songs were often called "The ___ ___ ___ ___ ___ ___ Songs."

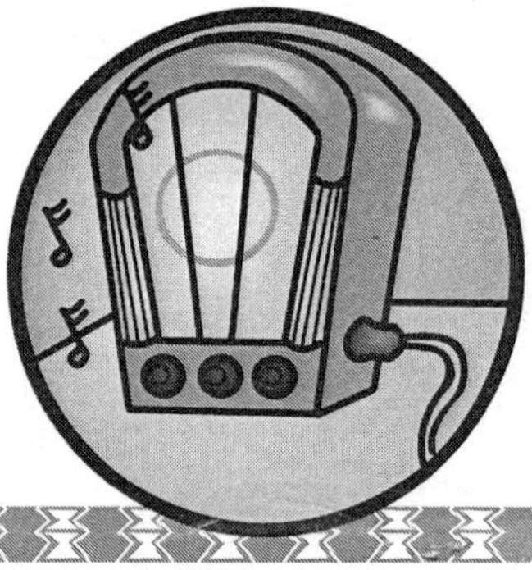

8. Nat King Cole was the first black to have his own ___ ___ ___ ___ ___ ___ ___ ___ ___ ___ show.

ANSWER BANK

Sorrow bop Orleans

wrote Duke folk

pianist television

Answers: 1. Duke; 2. pianist; 3. folk; 4. bop; 5. Orleans; 6. wrote; 7. Sorrow; 8. television

SING AN OLD SONG

The roots of black singing travel deep into history. The spirituals and gospel music come from Africa when the singing was performed in another language.

WAR SONG

O that Great Bird of War!
Thou hast made this town silent.
They come, they come
Creeping down low
Among the tall grasses,
The enemy come.

"Fare thee well,
Fare thee well,
On that far-off journey,
We shall carry thee to the hill."

"My child, lie, down,
Your mother's gone to the farm
So the Great Spirit will bear
You on his back."

"Witch, O great Witch,
You will take all bad children."

–OLD AFRICAN SONG

"Eonlay zeer marco
Eonlay yonga songa
Monga eonlay zeer
Marco way marco
Marco way marco
Mama."

"Nar ju pentee,
Nar de an mo ne clay
Key geelo ply
An moo moo Ken po –"

"Kan, Kan, O some bay, O,
An noo you Kan."

–OLD AFRICAN SONG

Get on board, little children
Get on board, little children
Get on board, little children
There's room for many a more.

– BLACK SPIRITUAL

Youthful tree!
We must cut all around it Gala's tree!
We must cut all around it
Cawlaw, Cawlaw, Cawlaw, Cawlaw.
We must cut around it.

–OLD AFRICAN SONG

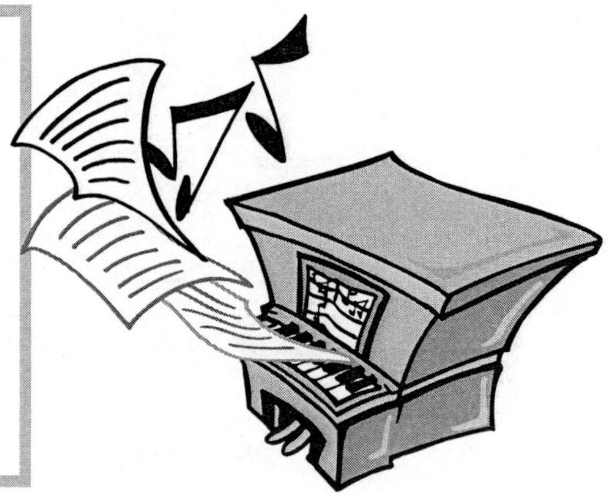

WRITE A NEW SONG

Make up a new song of your own!

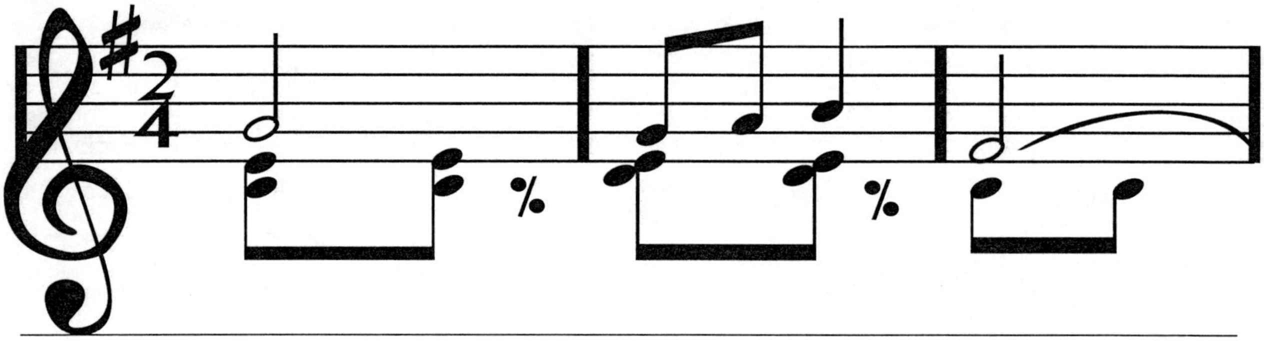

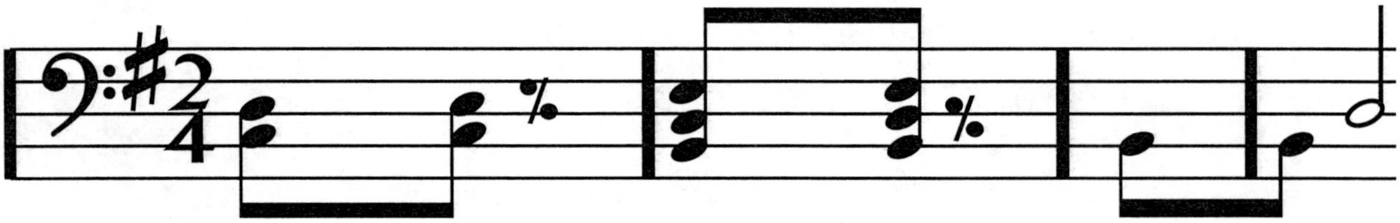

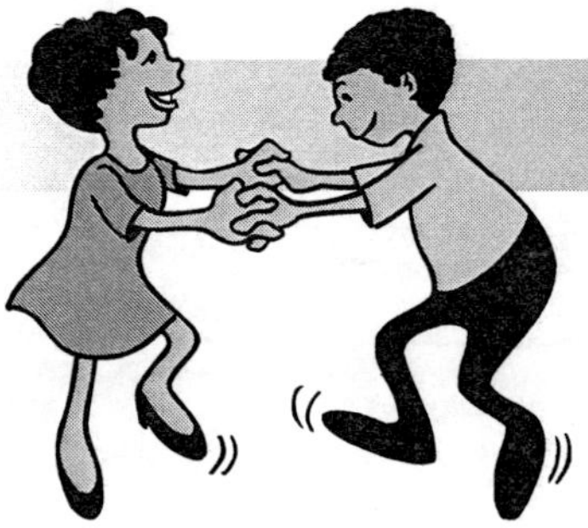

LET'S DANCE!

Invent a dance of your very own! Draw the steps below.

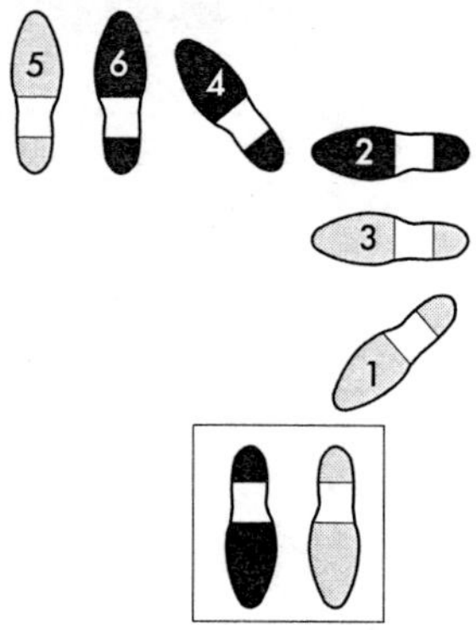

Write the name of your dance and what it represents below.

WRITE ABOUT IT!

Write an original story to read aloud. Use your most vivid imagination!

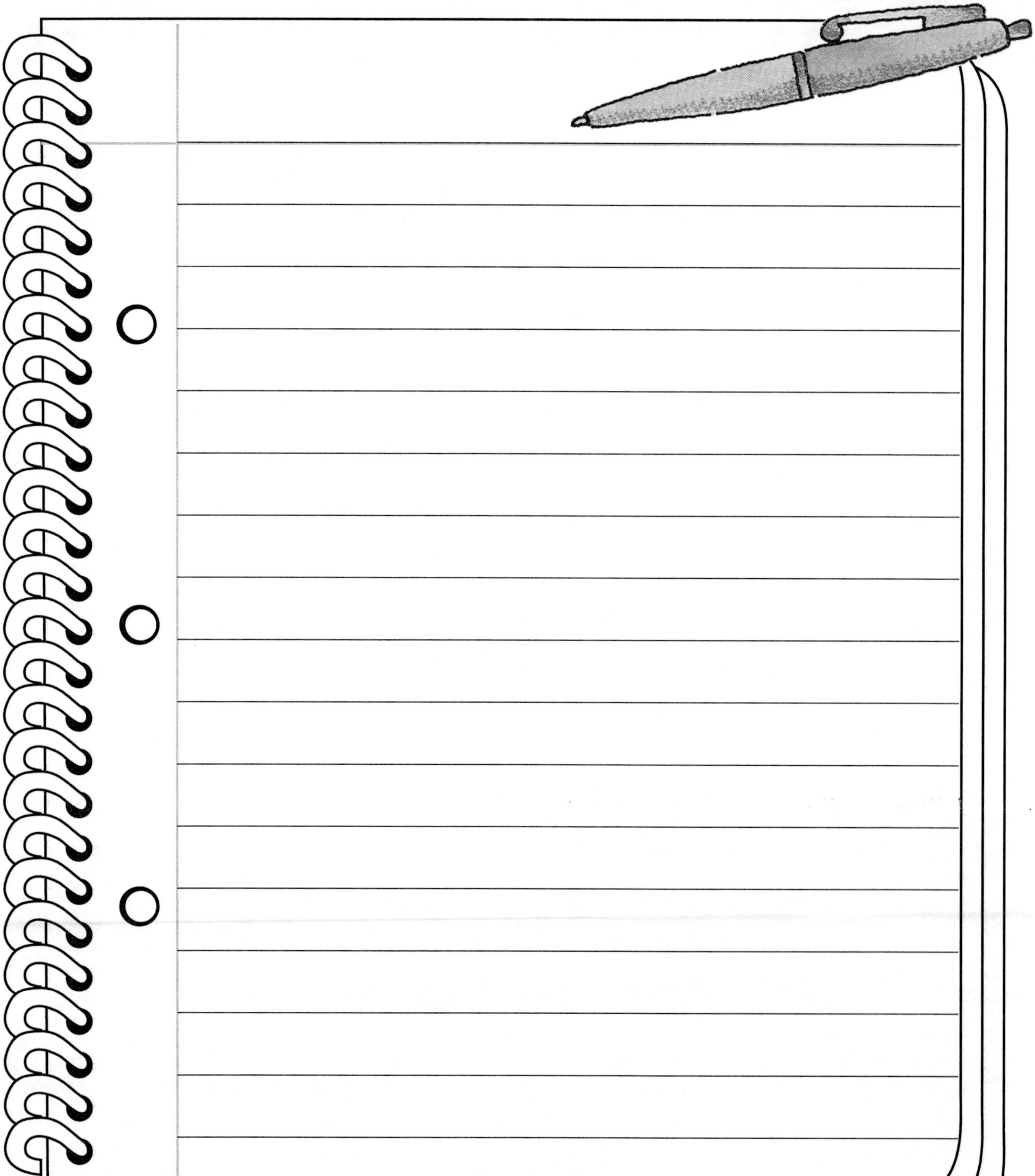

PUT IT IN STONE!

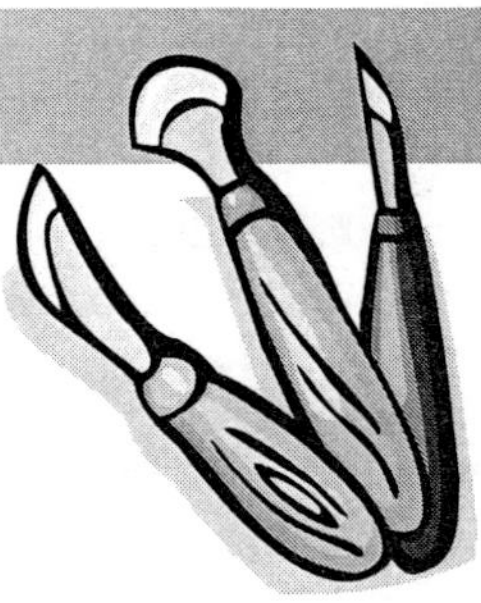

So you want to sculpt!

Draw the item that you plan to work on here!

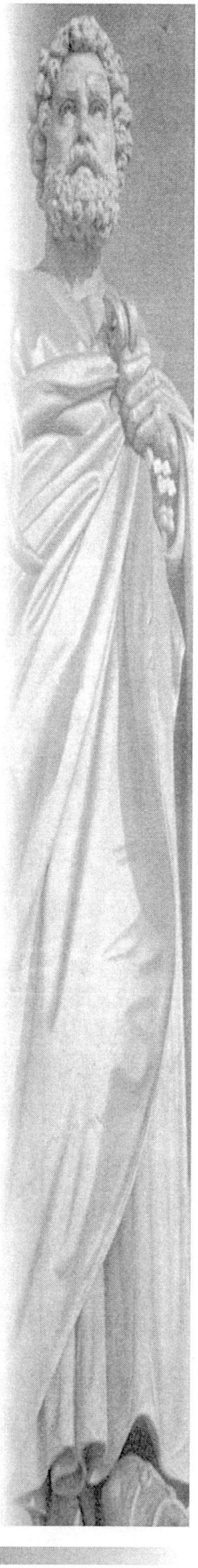

CREATE A MASTERPIECE!

Paint or draw your masterpiece! Once your are finished, host an art exhibit with your friends!

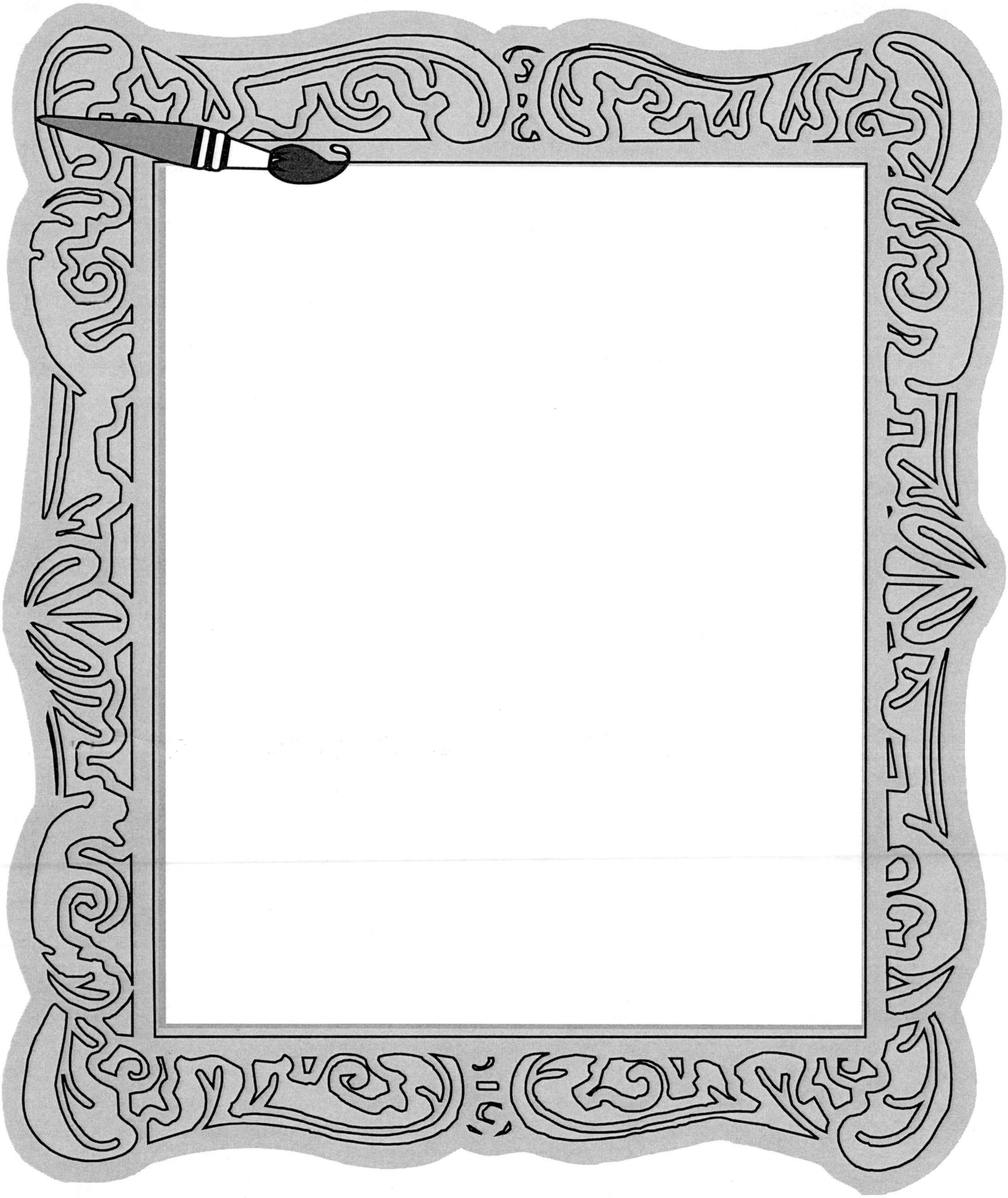

FAN MAIL!

Write a letter to your favorite person or persons in the arts. In your letter, you could ask questions about how they became successful and even for an autograph. Do some research using books, magazines, or the internet to find the right mailing address.

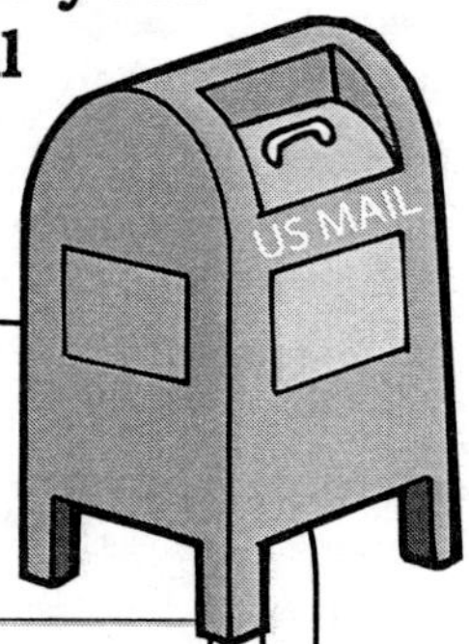

INDEX